Payton Finds a Friend

Dr. Gloria McDaniel-Hall

Illustrations by Ammar Yaqoub Yahya

Payton Finds a Friend

A book about Payton's adventures of going to a new school, making new connections, and learning important lessons!

Written by Gloria McDaniel-Hall

Illustrated by Ammar Yaqoub Yahya

Book design by Megan Stoneson

Published by Gloria McDaniel-Hall

Copyright © 2022 Gloria McDaniel-Hall

To request permissions, contact the publisher at glomc@hotmail.com

Paperback ISBN: 9798848717846

www.urbanlegendspd.com

Have you ever had to try something new - like going to a new school?
If it made you feel like you had butterflies in your tummy...this book is for YOU!

My name is Payton.

I'm 6 years old and I'm going to tell you a story about what happened to me when I had to leave kindergarten and go to first grade at a BRAND NEW SCHOOL!

I don't know if you've ever been afraid to do something new? I certainly was - well, at least at first I was!

I LOVED KINDERGARTEN!

I loved everything about it. I loved my teacher, my friends, my classroom, my principal, the books, and ALL MY CLASSES too.

Everyone was friendly and it kind of felt like being at home. Kindergarten is the place where I learned how exciting school really is. Ms. McGillen, my teacher, made learning so much fun. I wanted to be in her class FOREVER! She was a good teacher. She helped me learn SO MANY new things.

I had some best friends too! They liked to do the same things I liked to do at recess! My best BEST friends were Camille, Anthony, and Charles. We played all kinds of games together during recess.

When I got home at the end of every day, I'd pretend like I was the teacher with my "buddies" (I call them my buddies, most people call them stuffed animals) at home.

One of the best things about kindergarten was my friends!

I thought that good feeling would last forever....and then **IT** happened.

My mom and dad told me that I was going to have to change schools when I went to first grade. I was really happy to be going to a bigger grade, but I was really sad that I couldn't go to my same kindergarten school. I had to go to a big kid school, a brand new school. I got sad and asked my parents a lot of questions. My mom and dad did all the things parents should do (I guess) when they have to help kids get ready for a new school:

They called the new school for a visit.

I had about 100 questions - and they answered all of them!

They found out all about the supplies I needed.

They got my new uniforms.

Then they talked with me some more...

But it still wasn't okay! I MISSED KINDERGARTEN!

I MISSED ALL THE THINGS THAT I LOVED ABOUT MY OLD SCHOOL. I DIDN'T REALLY WANT TO GO TO A NEW SCHOOL!

I had lots of fun during the summer before first grade.
I went to camp and did lots of activities. I knew the day
was coming when all this fun would come to an end and
it would be time to start at my new school.

One day, right after camp was over, my mom and dad
took me to visit my new school. At first, I didn't even want
to walk inside! But because both of them were with me,
I knew it would be okay.

When I first saw my new school, it looked really big and
a little scary. I didn't know where anything was. I didn't
know where my classroom was. I didn't know who my
teacher was. Where is the bathroom?!!!

We stopped in the office and there were really nice
people there. They told us how to find my new room.
It was Room 125!

I had so many questions!

Would my new teacher be nice?

Would the other children be nice?

Would we have fun like we did in kindergarten?

Would there be Mo Willems' books in the classroom library? I love Mo Willems!

Would I learn new things that were interesting?

Would my art and music classes be fun?

Would I be able to find my way around?

But the most important question was...
WOULD I BE ABLE TO FIND NEW FRIENDS?

My new teacher's name was Ms. Goldbury. She invited us into the room to talk. There weren't any kids there yet, just me and my family. While she talked with my parents, she let me look around the room. AND GUESS WHAT I SAW?

I saw books written by my favorite author, Mo Willems! I saw *Elephant and Piggie Let's Go For a Drive* and even more! This was turning out to be a good visit! Maybe first grade was going to be okay after all.

We said goodbye to Ms. Goldbury and went to the store to get the supplies on my list. We got all kinds of cool things like new crayons, big kid paper (not the kind with the 3 lines that we used in kindergarten), pencils, a new backpack and SO MUCH MORE. School shopping is the best!

We got home and put my name on everything and packed it all in my new backpack. There were two weeks before I started my new school. I was feeling better about this whole thing even though I still really missed everyone and everything about my old school. I don't really like new things that much. It feels a lot better when things stay JUST THE WAY THEY ARE! When things stay just the way they are, I know what to expect; when things change it can be a little scary!

There's something I really like about doing things the way I've always done them. I like when I get the same things for breakfast, lunch AND dinner. I even like when we read the same books at bedtime.

I guess sometimes things do have to change though.

Everyday, my parents talked with me about how the first day of school would be. They talked with me about how I needed to give it a try. They told me that I would be able to find new friends because that was still what I was most worried about. They kept telling me that my teacher would be nice and that I would be learning a lot of new things.

I asked if it would be okay to bring one of my "buddies" with me just in case. Mom said that I wouldn't be able to because that was one of the rules for first grade. NO STUFFED ANIMALS WERE ALLOWED!

What?! No stuffed animals?!

Mom and dad wouldn't even be able to come into my classroom with me on that first day to make sure I was okay. They had to drop me off in front and then I had to go in with my class.

What?! Drop me off at the front?!

This was so scary. Every time I thought about it, I got the feeling that butterflies were flying around in my tummy again!

This was going to be hard - REALLY hard.

I had to go to a new school.

I had to not show that I was frightened.

I had to learn a lot of new rules and other things.

And I had to do it all on my own because

I DIDN'T HAVE ANY FRIENDS AT THIS SCHOOL!

On the night before the first day we were busy getting everything ready.

Uniform - CHECK!

Favorite things packed in my lunch - CHECK!

All my supplies in my bag - CHECK!

Favorite buddies in bed - CHECK!

Dreaming about the new school - OF COURSE I WAS!

Then it finally came....

THE FIRST DAY OF FIRST GRADE!

Mom woke me up right on time. She had everything ready, including my favorite breakfast: bacon, raisin toast, and lots of strawberries! I was feeling like this was all going to be okay!

We made sure that I had all my things loaded in the car.

I was feeling kind of brave! I kept telling myself "YOU CAN DO THIS"....and then we pulled up in front of the school and it was time for me to jump out and join my class. And wouldn't you know it? Those butterflies came back.

Last week, it felt like there were about 10 of them in my tummy, but now - there were at least 100!

Those butterflies were flying all around, doing loops and somersaults! I was really scared. It was all so different. I DIDN'T KNOW ANY OF THESE PEOPLE except MS. Goldbury - and I didn't really know her. I had only met her once.

I didn't want to get out of the car.

I didn't want to go to this school.

I don't like new things.

I DON'T HAVE ANY FRIENDS HERE!

Having at least one friend would have made this so much better!

But, I gathered all my courage and I DID IT! I got out of the car and joined my line.

When we got into our classroom, Ms. Goldbury showed us all where to sit. We all had to listen quietly, with our eyes on her, while she explained where everything was and the rules of our classroom. There was so much to do and so many things to learn that it was lunch and recess time before I knew it.

I was almost feeling calm, but this was the part of the day that I was worried about. Most of the people in my class had all gone to school together before. When we got to our table in the lunchroom, it seemed like everybody knew somebody but me. I felt really sad. I wanted to talk to Camille, Anthony and Charles!

Then we went out on the playground. Everybody started running around and playing different games, I didn't feel like I could join in, so I just played a game by myself.

I wanted to go home. I wanted to let my mom and dad know that I didn't think this was going to work.

After recess, I just went to my seat and quietly did my work.

I was still really unhappy when my dad picked me up. He asked about my day. I told him about everyone knowing everybody but that nobody knew me. I told him that I played alone and made up my own game at recess. He told me that he was sure things would get better soon. Dad said, "Sometimes, things seem like they will never work out, but they almost always do."

That didn't make it better. I was really sad that evening.

The next morning, it was still hard to get out of the car - but I knew I had to do it. I went in with my class and went to my desk. But then something really good happened! Ms. Goldbury told me that I would be sitting in a new spot, next to Ruby. She said that Ruby was really a great helper and that she could help me all day. Ms. Goldbury said that Ruby was patient and that she liked helping people who needed it.

Ruby showed me where all the Mo Willems' books were!

She helped me with a couple of my math problems (she was really good at her two times tables)!

She let me sit next to her at lunch!

She introduced me to two other friends, Kasey and Melanie. Then, guess what?

They all played with me when we went outside to recess!

We played a special game of tag!

I can run fast so it was hard for them to catch me - and they didn't even get upset.

We had so much fun that none of us wanted to go inside when recess was over!

This morning I had no friends and then by the end of the day, I HAD 3 NEW FRIENDS.

I couldn't wait to tell mom when I got in the car after school. I told her about EVERYTHING! I told her about my new seat, about all the ways Ruby helped me, about my new friends Kasey and Melanie, about our tag game. I even told her about how nobody could catch me at recess.

It only took a few days, but things were looking up.

I had friends to learn and play with every day!

And guess what else? The butterflies were almost ALL gone. There are still a few new things that I had to get used to, but I think there will always be something new. If I just learn to get help when I need it, it seems like things almost always turn out to be okay in the end!

PAYTON'S TOP TEN LESSONS 10 ABOUT DOING NEW THINGS

So when you feel those butterflies....

Take it from me! Here are a few lessons I learned. I call them Payton's Top Ten Lessons for times that things seem new and scary:

1. New things will happen to us all the time.

2. It's okay for us to be a little scared of new things sometimes. Everybody gets a few butterflies every now and then.

3. We should talk about how we feel with someone like mom, dad, grandma, or auntie.

4. A lot of times we make problems bigger (in our heads) than they really are.

5. You won't be the only one feeling lonely and nervous.

6. Great teachers know how to make us feel welcome.

7. Just because we don't play with everybody doesn't mean they couldn't become our friends.

8. New places can mean new chances to grow.

9. It's okay to be the first one to say hi.

10. Most people are really nice when you get to know them.

Dear parents and guardians!

There are so many things that can be difficult about helping your child transition to a new environment (especially school). Your primary goal should be to help your child ease into the transition so it can feel as smooth as possible. There are lots of ideas in *Payton Finds a Friend*! A few of them are listed here. Use these tips to reduce the stress your child might face when there are new situations.

1. Ask questions.

2. Go visit the new school and get to know the staff.

3. Talk about times things were hard for you and discuss ways you got through them.

4. Be patient.

5. Keep as many things "the same" as you can during transitions.

6. Read other books about children who have navigated new or difficult situations.

7. Reassure your child that everyone feels a bit frightened about new things at times.

8. Stay in touch with former acquaintances if possible.

9. Find unique ways for your child to process what's happening - like through journaling!

10. Just be there. Let your little one know that "you got them."

Following are a few sample questions you can use to start the conversation with your child about new transitions. Talking about it always makes everything feel better!

1. How are you feeling about going to (insert the new place) or doing (insert the new thing your child is trying)?

2. If your friend was worried about doing something new, what advice would you give him or her?

3. What is one thing you are really worried about?

4. What was something that went well the last time you tried something new?

5. Would you like to practice (whatever the new experience is) with me?

Dear Teachers!

We all know it is vitally important that students feel psychologically safe in our classrooms and in our schools. There are typically so many things happening at once in schools that it's easy to forget the importance of building and fostering relationships. It's such a scary thing to be the new one in a classroom - at the beginning of the year or if you transfer in after school has started. I know you have strategies that you use to help your students ease into the transition. There are lots of ideas in *Payton Finds a Friend* and a few more are listed below. Use these tips to reduce the stress for new students and make sure to send ideas of things that have worked so that we can put our thoughts together to create a collective of care for new students.

1. Create a sense of belonging for students and their families. For example, make personal calls home if time allows. In the era of texts, real voices make such a difference.

2. Explain your procedures to students and families and share the "why" behind things - like "We don't think it's a good idea for parents to come into the room at the beginning of the year because it's really hard on students when parents have to leave."

3. Invite new parents and students to visit your classroom before the school year begins, if possible.

4. Create opportunities for students to help each other.

5. Create leadership opportunities for students, i.e. "class ambassador" (make a big deal about this too).

6. Create opportunities to help new students get acquainted with procedures and other important things to know about your classroom and the school.

7. Find out as much as possible about students' interests and add connections for them in your room (i.e. add high interest books into your library, using writing prompts which align with things students like to do, etc.).

8. Make sure that during social times (i.e. lunch, recess, etc.), you notice and attend to any student who seems alone (unless they are choosing some alone time).

9. Ask your colleagues to share effective strategies they have successfully used.

10. Set up expectations (along with students) emphasizing sharing, caring and making everyone feel welcome.

Social-Emotional learning (SEL) Resources/Websites:

- **CASEL,** Social Emotional Learning Collective: https://casel.org/

- **The Sped Guru,** Parent Support: https://thespedguru.com/category/parent-support/

- **Edutopia,** Social & Emotional Learning (SEL): https://www.edutopia.org/social-emotional-learning

- **EMOTIONAL,** Empowering Children with Better Emotional Skills: https://www.emotionalabcs.com/

- **Flocabulary,** Social & Emotional Learning: https://www.flocabulary.com/topics/social-and-emotional-learning/

> "I've learned that people will forget what you said, people will forget what you did, but people will never forget how you made them feel."
>
> –Maya Angelou

This page is dedicated to my amazing friends who supported this project and who continue to support me in so many ways. I love you and couldn't do this work without each and every one of you! I will never forget how you make me feel!

Sincerely,

Gloria

Beth Blair	Dr. Lawrence Powell
Dr. Landon Brown	Dr. Megan Quaile
Rachel Douglas-Swanson	Constance Roberts
Erika Flynn	Denise Ruffin
Eric Gibson, Jr.	Angela K. Sherrill
Janice Glaspie	Michael Stack
Omar Hameen	Nena and Ryan Szczepanski
Alan and Connie Harper	Jesse Tang
Eboni Haynes	Gabriela Waschewsky
Darrell Johnson	Craig Wilson
Desiree Kirton	Gary Wilson
Monica McCullough	Stephanie Wise-Cunningham
Heather Pittman	Dwayne Wooten

Made in the USA
Monee, IL
22 March 2023